GLADIATOR

Written by
GLEN DOWNEY

Illustrated by
ANDREW BARR

This story is set in ancient Rome. Some of the characters and events are fictional, but others are real. Each chapter ends with a non-fiction page that gives more information about real people's lives and actual events in ancient Rome.

OXFORD
UNIVERSITY PRESS

MARCUS SILANUS

AURELIUS

COMMODUS

SICARIUS MAXIMUS

CAIUS PROCURUS

LAVINIA

REAL PEOPLE IN HISTORY

AURELIUS (AD/CE **121–180**): The Roman Emperor from AD/CE 169–180, Aurelius was a good emperor who disliked gladiator contests.

COMMODUS (AD/CE **161–192**): Son of Aurelius, Commodus was a great fan of gladiator fighting and organised many games.

FICTIONAL CHARACTERS

MARCUS SILANUS: A 14-year-old boy who is forced into slavery and becomes a gladiator.

SICARIUS MAXIMUS: A cruel Roman gladiator who kills Marcus' father.

CAIUS PROCURUS: An owner of gladiators, who trains Marcus to fight for his life.

LAVINIA: The mother of Marcus. She is put in prison for debt after her husband's death.

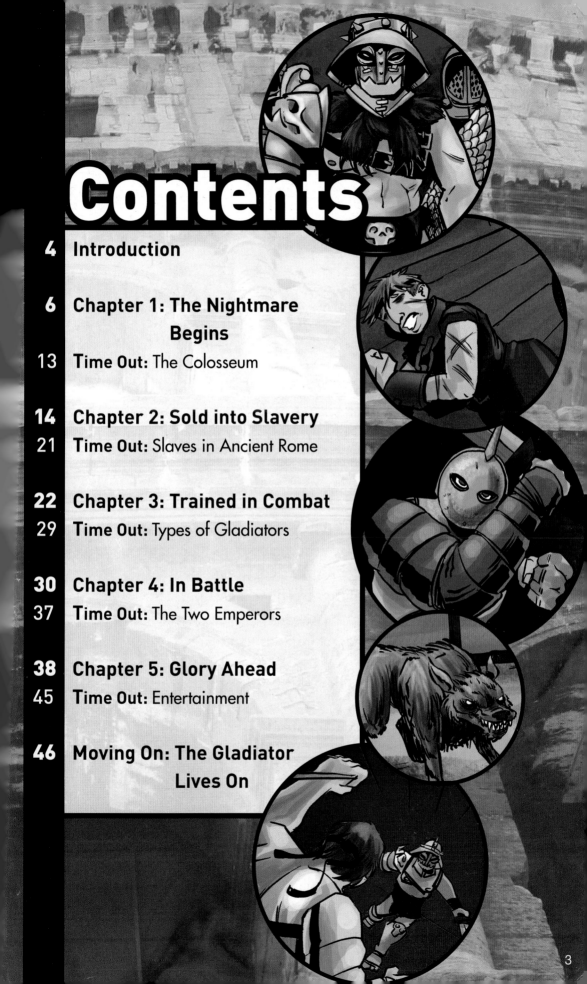

Contents

4 Introduction

6 Chapter 1: The Nightmare
Begins
13 Time Out: The Colosseum

14 Chapter 2: Sold into Slavery
21 Time Out: Slaves in Ancient Rome

22 Chapter 3: Trained in Combat
29 Time Out: Types of Gladiators

30 Chapter 4: In Battle
37 Time Out: The Two Emperors

38 Chapter 5: Glory Ahead
45 Time Out: Entertainment

46 Moving On: The Gladiator
Lives On

Pollice Verso (Thumbs Down)
by Jean-Léon Gérôme, 1872

Long before professional boxing and wrestling, the citizens of Rome watched fighting spectacles at the largest arena in the city, the Colosseum. The fighters were gladiators – men who battled to the death for fame, glory and the chance of freedom. The Emperors of Rome would pay for these events as a way of keeping their subjects happy and entertained.

TIMELINE

The letters BCE stand for 'Before Common Era'. The years before the Common Era are counted backwards, so the greater the number, the longer ago it was. For example, 310 BCE is further in the past than 65 BCE.

310 BC/BCE »	264 BC/BCE »	65 BC/BCE »	AD/CE 70 »	AD/CE 80 »
The first recorded gladiator games take place in southern Italy.	The first gladiator games in Rome take place at a funeral. The games are put on to honour the dead.	Julius Caesar builds an amphitheatre for gladiator contests.	Construction of the Colosseum in Rome begins during the reign of Emperor Vespasian.	The Colosseum is completed. It hosts the first games.

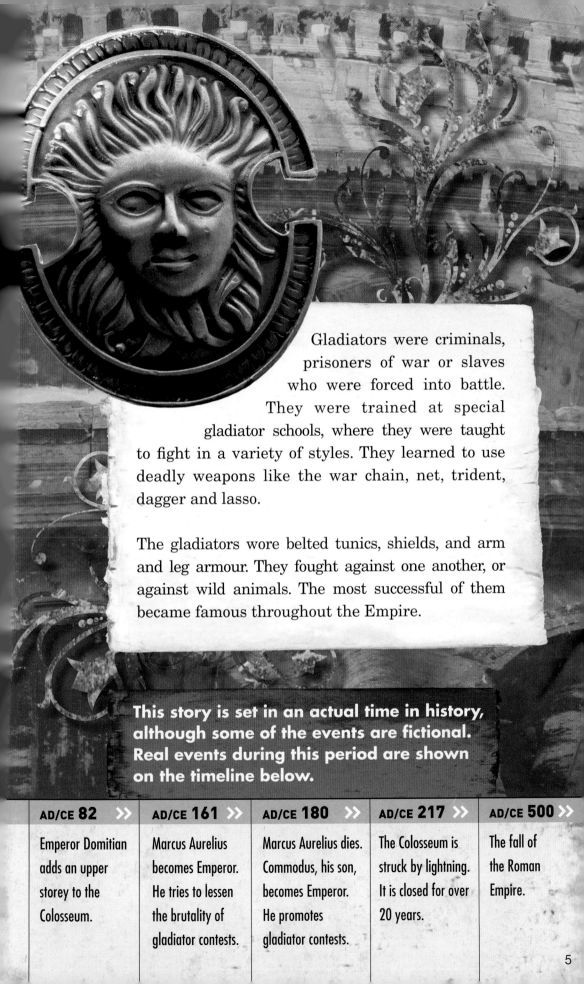

Gladiators were criminals, prisoners of war or slaves who were forced into battle. They were trained at special gladiator schools, where they were taught to fight in a variety of styles. They learned to use deadly weapons like the war chain, net, trident, dagger and lasso.

The gladiators wore belted tunics, shields, and arm and leg armour. They fought against one another, or against wild animals. The most successful of them became famous throughout the Empire.

This story is set in an actual time in history, although some of the events are fictional. Real events during this period are shown on the timeline below.

AD/CE 82 »	AD/CE 161 »	AD/CE 180 »	AD/CE 217 »	AD/CE 500 »
Emperor Domitian adds an upper storey to the Colosseum.	Marcus Aurelius becomes Emperor. He tries to lessen the brutality of gladiator contests.	Marcus Aurelius dies. Commodus, his son, becomes Emperor. He promotes gladiator contests.	The Colosseum is struck by lightning. It is closed for over 20 years.	The fall of the Roman Empire.

CHAPTER I: The Nightmare Begins

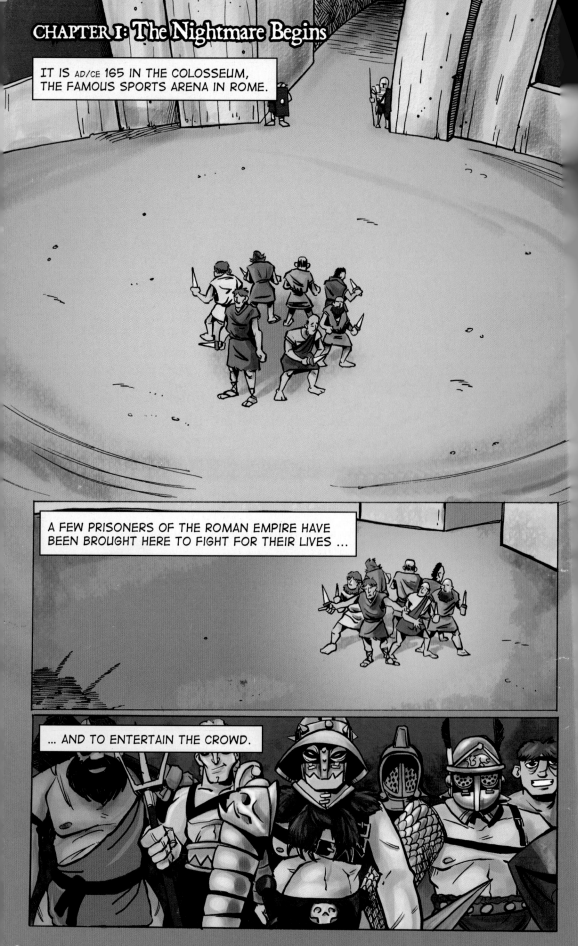

IT IS AD/CE 165 IN THE COLOSSEUM, THE FAMOUS SPORTS ARENA IN ROME.

A FEW PRISONERS OF THE ROMAN EMPIRE HAVE BEEN BROUGHT HERE TO FIGHT FOR THEIR LIVES ...

... AND TO ENTERTAIN THE CROWD.

TEN YEARS LATER, TITUS' SON MARCUS WAKES UP FROM A NIGHTMARE ABOUT HIS FATHER'S DEATH.

HE STILL REMEMBERS THE DAY WHEN SOLDIERS CAME TO TAKE HIS FATHER AWAY.

IT HAPPENED 10 YEARS AGO ...

ARE YOU TITUS SILANUS?

YES. WHAT'S ALL THIS?

BY ORDER OF EMPEROR AURELIUS, I HEREBY ARREST YOU FOR MAKING WEAPONS FOR ENEMIES OF ROME.

BUT ... THE WEAPONS I MAKE ARE JUST FOR HUNTING!

SILENCE! LET'S GO.

FATHER!

The Colosseum

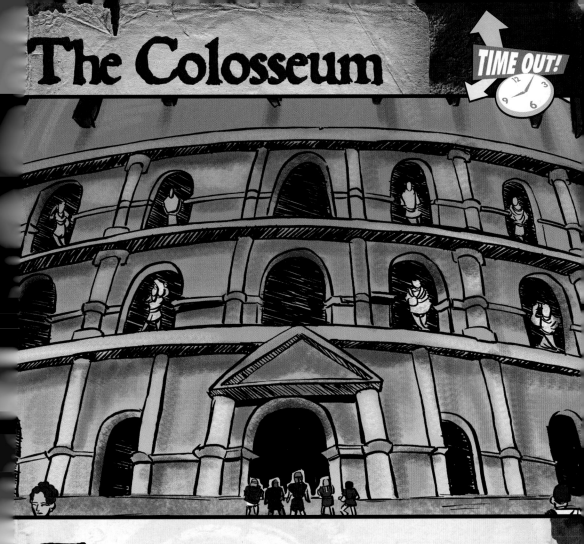

The Colosseum was one of the most well-known buildings of the ancient world. It was a huge, oval-shaped stadium. It seated up to 75,000 spectators!

The building was nearly 50 metres high, taller than the Statue of Liberty. The arena was over 3,000 square metres in area, nearly twice the size of an ice skating rink.

Romans went to the Colosseum to watch gladiator contests and chariot races. Sometimes the arena was flooded with water and battles involving actual warships were staged!

When gladiator battles were no longer held after AD/CE 404, the killing of wild animals became popular. Elephants, lions, bears, hyenas and panthers were killed in front of cheering spectators. At other times, a condemned criminal would be thrown to the wild beasts.

HALF ASLEEP ...

IT'S BEEN TWO DAYS. THEY MUST HAVE GIVEN HIM A BIG WHACK!

HE'LL WAKE UP SOON.

SLOWLY, MARCUS OPENS HIS EYES.

MARCUS REALISES HE IS A SLAVE.

W-WHAT'S HAPPENED? WHERE AM I?

15

Slaves in Ancient Rome

TIME OUT!

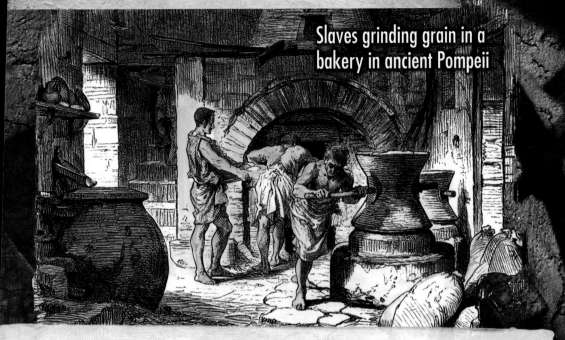

Slaves grinding grain in a bakery in ancient Pompeii

As the Roman armies swept across Europe and North Africa, they often made slaves of the people they conquered. Slaves were regarded as personal property. They were bought and sold like livestock. They could not marry or own anything. They provided free labour for their owners and lived under extremely harsh conditions. Many people killed themselves rather than be taken as slaves.

Some Roman households kept hundreds of slaves. It has been estimated that up to a third of people living in the Roman Empire were slaves.

Perhaps the most famous Roman slave was a gladiator named Spartacus. From 73–71 BC/BCE, Spartacus led thousands of slaves against the Roman armies. However, Spartacus and his men were defeated.

Spartacus, a gladiator slave

Types of Gladiators

Gladiators were trained at special schools in different styles of fighting. Each style had its own weapons.

Retiarius (net man)
He carried a net in his right hand and a trident, or three-pronged fork, in his left.

Dimachaerus (two-knife man)
He carried a short sword in each hand.

Bestiarus (animal man)
He fought against wild animals like lions and bears.

Laquearius (lasso man)
He used a noose or lasso to catch his opponent.

CHAPTER 4: In Battle

MARCUS HURLS HIS SPEAR ...

AARGH!!

THE WINNER IS ... MARCUS THE HUNTER!

ONE DAY, I WILL BEAT SICARIUS ...

YOU HAVE EARNED THE CHANCE TO PROVE YOURSELF, MARCUS.

THANK YOU, CAIUS.

I MEAN TO WIN FREEDOM FOR MYSELF ... AND FOR MY MOTHER.

VERY GOOD, MY BOY.

MARCUS CONTINUES TO TRAIN AND COMPETE ...

FOR HIS HONOUR ...

... AND FOR HIS FREEDOM.

HE GROWS IN SKILL AND STRENGTH.

I HAVE SOME NEWS.
EMPEROR AURELIUS IS PLANNING A SERIES OF GAMES IN THE COLOSSEUM.
I HAVE CHOSEN THREE OF YOU TO TAKE PART. WHO KNOWS? YOU MAY EVEN WIN YOUR FREEDOM ...
"AARON THE WARRIOR ... "
"WIGLAF THE BARBARIAN ..."
"AND MARCUS THE HUNTER."
IF YOU WIN THIS TOURNAMENT, MARCUS, YOU MAY WIN MORE THAN YOUR FREEDOM.
WHAT DO YOU MEAN?
THE EMPEROR WILL GRANT THE WINNER ONE REQUEST.
FREEDOM FOR MY MOTHER!

The Two Emperors

Marcus Aurelius (AD/CE 121–180) was Emperor of Rome from AD/CE 161 until his death. Born of a noble family, he was a kind and serious ruler. He was interested in philosophy, and wrote a book called *Meditations* about his thoughts on life and leadership.

Emperor Marcus Aurelius

During his reign, Aurelius reformed Roman laws to make life easier for people such as widows, slaves and minors. The time of his rule is regarded as the Golden Age of the Roman Empire.

Commodus

By contrast, Aurelius' son Commodus (AD/CE 161–192) was one of the worst Roman emperors. Many believe that he was insane. He often took part in gladiator contests dressed up as Hercules, the Greek god and hero. In AD/CE 192, his advisers had him assassinated.

CHAPTER 5: Glory Ahead

THE DAY OF THE GAMES ARRIVES.

REMEMBER, GLADIATORS, IT IS IMPORTANT TO WIN QUICKLY AND TO SAVE YOUR STRENGTH.

YES, BUT ALSO ...

WE KNOW, CAIUS — IT'S IMPORTANT TO *ENTERTAIN*.

LET'S SEE WHERE THEY ARE IN THE PROGRAMME.

Entertainment

TIME OUT!

The tradition of fighting as a test of skill or as entertainment did not die with the Romans in ancient times. In the Middle Ages, European knights participated in tournaments in which they competed in the joust (which involved knocking an opponent off his horse with a lance) and in hand-to-hand combat (with swords, maces and other weapons). Like the gladiators of ancient Rome, the knights could be badly injured or even killed, but they entertained the crowds and were very popular.

Today, sports such as boxing, wrestling, rugby or football are popular forms of entertainment. In many ways, sports fans are like the ancient Romans. They like to have heroes to cheer for and opponents to yell at. They enjoy watching competitors with different skills and abilities face off against one another.

MOVING ON

The Gladiator Lives On

For almost 700 years, Roman audiences were entertained by gladiators in combat. Many gladiators lost their lives in front of cheering crowds.

The Roman audiences were also entertained by animals. It is thought that the trapping of animals for these sports caused the extinction of some animal species.

These contests seem very brutal to us today, but the Romans were inspired by the skill and bravery of the gladiators. They portrayed gladiators in paintings, pottery and sculpture. They also wrote about gladiators in books.

The age of gladiators came to an end when Emperor Constantine, a Christian, banned gladiator contests in AD/CE 325. In AD/CE 399, gladiator schools were closed by Emperor Honorius. The games were abolished for good in AD/CE 404.

Scene from the
movie *Spartacus*

Tourists visiting the ruins of
the Colosseum in Rome

Today, tourists from all over the world visit
the ruins of the Colosseum in Rome. Movies
about gladiators, such as *Spartacus* (1960)
and *Gladiator* (2000), are box-office hits.

Scene from the
movie *Gladiator*

INDEX

A
Africa, 21
Amphitheatre, 4
Aurelius, Emperor Marcus, 5, 37

B
Bestiarus, 29

C
Caesar, Julius, 4
Colosseum, 4–5, 13, 47
Commodus, 5, 37
Constantine, Emperor, 46

D
Dimachaerus, 29
Domitian, Emperor, 5

E
Europe, 21

G
Gladiator(s), 4–5, 29

H
Hercules, 37
Honorius, Emperor, 46

I
Italy, 4

L
Laquearius, 29

M
Meditations, 37

O
Octavius of Gaul, 41–42

R
Retiarius, 29
Roman Empire, 5–6, 21, 37, 45
Rome, 4, 47

S
Slave(s), 5, 21
Spartacus, 21, 47
Statue of Liberty, 13

V
Vespasian, Emperor, 4

GLOSSARY

Colosseum – a huge stadium where gladiator contests were held

combat – to fight

entertain – to perform in front of an audience to amuse them

gladiator – a man trained to fight for public amusement in ancient Rome

opponent – a person against another in a contest

prey – an animal or person who is hunted by another

slave – a person who is owned by another person and works without being paid

spectator – a person who watches a contest or game

train – to practise, especially for a sporting event

warrior – a person who fights in a battle